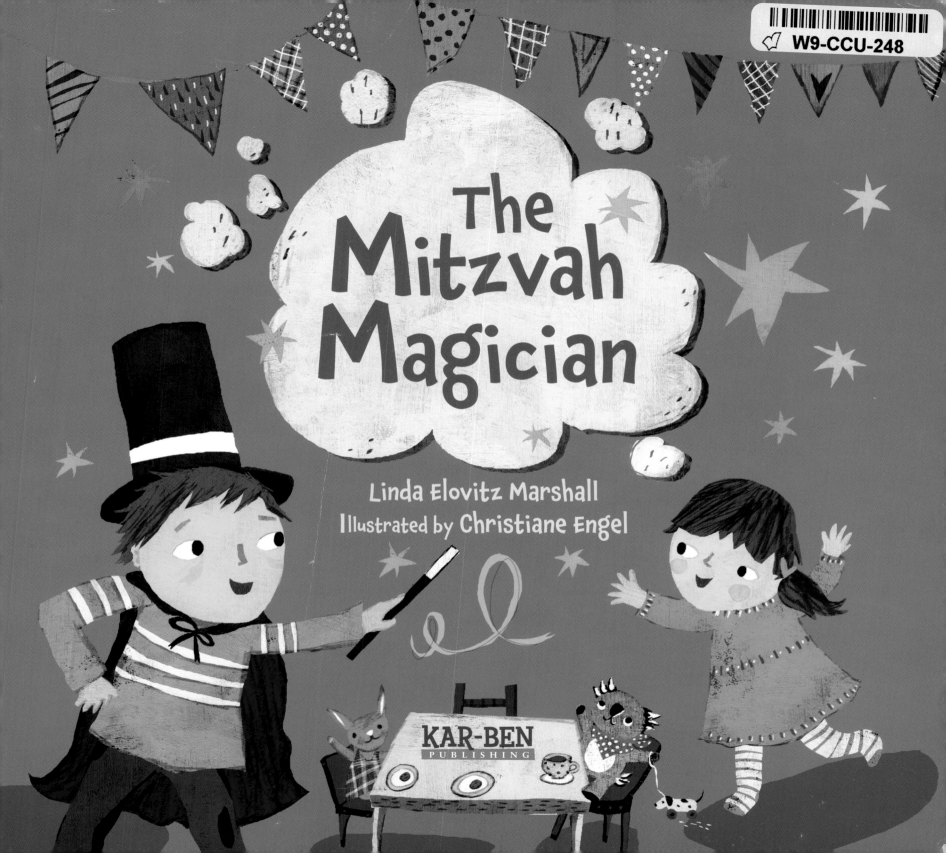

The Mitzvah Magician

Linda Elovitz Marshall

Illustrated by Christiane Engel

KAR-BEN
PUBLISHING

To my current-and-future grandchildren
Gabriel, Niomi, Julia, Lyra, Avi, Talia, Leah, Noa, and Baruch
for their wonderful mitzvot . . . and their magic. — L.E.M.

For Beverly — C. E.

Text copyright © 2012 by LInda Elovitz Marshall
Illustrations copyright © 2012 Lerner Publishing Group, Inc.

KAR-BEN PUBLISHING, INC.
A division of Lerner Publishing Group, Inc.
241 First Avenue North
Minneapolis, MN 55401 U.S.A.
1-800-4-Karben

Website address: www.karben.com

Library of Congress Cataloging-in-Publication Data

Marshall, Linda Elovitz.
   The Mitzvah Magician / by Linda Elovitz Marshall ; illustrated by Christiane Engel.
      p.   cm.
      Summary: Gabriel's first attempt at magic lands him in time out, but then he
follows his mother's advice to use magic to do good deeds, surprising her and his little sister.
      ISBN: 978-0-7613-5655-4 (lib. bdg : alk. paper)
      [1. Magic tricks—Fiction. 2. Commandments (Judaism)—Fiction. 3. Jews—Fiction.]
   I. Engel, Christiane, ill. II. Title.
   PZ7.M35672453Mit 2012
   [E]—dc23   2011029818

Manufactured in the United States of America
1 – CG – 5/1/13

071318K1

This
PJ BOOK
belongs to

_____

_____

PjLibrary®

JEWISH BEDTIME STORIES and SONGS

The very first time Gabriel wore his magician's cape and hat, he waved his magic wand and said his magic words.

"PRESTO MAGICO! I'm Gabriel the Great Magician! Glass, be empty!" he commanded.

He waved his magic wand near the glass. Milk spilled all over the counter and all over the floor. Soon the glass was empty.

Gabriel waved his magic wand again.
He waved it so close to his little
sister Julia that it poked her
in the tummy.

"**PRESTO MAGICO!** I'm Gabriel the Great Magician.
I can make you disappear."

But Julia didn't disappear. She cried.

"**Time Out!**" ordered Gabriel's mother. "You need to sit on the stool until you can behave."

"But I'm Gabriel the Great Magician," he insisted. "I need to wave my magic wand."

"Gabriel, good magicians aren't mean. Good magicians do things that make people happy, not sad. They do mitzvot—that's a Jewish word for good deeds," said his mother.

Gabriel sat on the stool, stomped his feet, and yelled, "I didn't mean to be mean. I'm a magician! I'm Gabriel the Great!"

"If you don't settle down," said his mother, "I'll have to take away your cape and hat and magic wand. I'm counting to three. One ... Two ..."

Gabriel got quiet.

His mother scooped up Julia and left the room.

Gabriel thought, "To make mitzvot, I need new magic words. I need Jewish words."

He waved his magic wand. "I wish I had new magic words," he said. "One-wish! Two-wish!"

He sneaked off the stool.
He tiptoed into the kitchen.

He waved his magic wand. "One-wish! Two-wish! **JEW-WISH!**" he exclaimed. "Kitchen, be clean!"

He put down his magic wand and wiped the counter and mopped the floor.

Then he rushed back to the stool.

He thought and thought some more.

He sneaked off the stool again and tiptoed into the living room. He waved his magic wand.

"One-wish! Two-wish! **JEW-WISH!**" he commanded, "Toys, be tidy!"

He put down his magic wand, picked up the toys, and put them in the toy box.

Then he rushed back to the stool.

He thought and thought and thought some more.

He sneaked off the stool a third time.
He set the table for his mother, Julia, and
himself. He put a cookie on each plate.

Then he set plates and cookies on Julia's doll table, too.

He rushed back to the stool.

He was just in time. His mother and Julia were coming down the stairs.

"Are you ready to behave?" his mother asked.

Gabriel waved his magic wand over his head.

"Yes, Mommy," he answered. "I'm Gabriel the Great and I have new magic words. I can do mitzvot."

"Good," she said. "But first let's clean up the mess you made in the kitchen."

"Watch," said Gabriel.

He waved his magic wand.
He said his magic words,

"One-wish! Two-wish! JEW-WISH!
Kitchen, be clean!"

His mother looked into the kitchen. It was very clean.

"How did that happen?" she asked.

Gabriel waved his magic wand again. He said his magic words.

"One-wish! Two-wish! JEW-WISH!
Toys, be tidy!"

His mother looked into the living room. All the toys were in the toy box.

"Wow!" she said.

Gabriel waved his magic wand a third time and said,

"One-wish! Two-wish! JEW-WISH! Cookies, be ready!"

He smiled, pointed to the tables, and took a deep bow.

Julia clapped, and his mother gave him a big hug.

"I make mitzvot," he announced.

"I'm Gabriel the Great. I'm the Mitzvah Magician!"

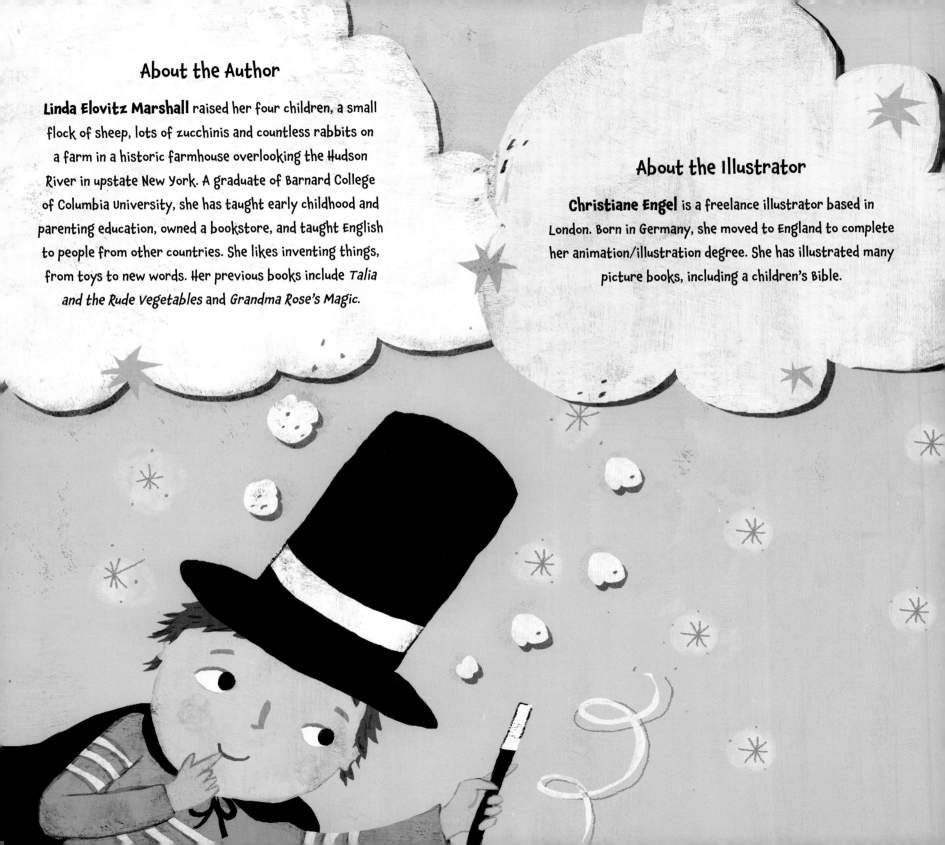

About the Author

Linda Elovitz Marshall raised her four children, a small flock of sheep, lots of zucchinis and countless rabbits on a farm in a historic farmhouse overlooking the Hudson River in upstate New York. A graduate of Barnard College of Columbia University, she has taught early childhood and parenting education, owned a bookstore, and taught English to people from other countries. She likes inventing things, from toys to new words. Her previous books include *Talia and the Rude Vegetables* and *Grandma Rose's Magic*.

About the Illustrator

Christiane Engel is a freelance illustrator based in London. Born in Germany, she moved to England to complete her animation/illustration degree. She has illustrated many picture books, including a children's Bible.